HUBBLE BUBBLE

The GLORIOUS GRANNY BAKE OFF!

TRACEY CORDEROY

JOE BERGER

nosy crow

First published in the UK in 2013 by Nosy Crow Ltd
The Crow's Nest, 14 Baden Place, Crosby Row
London, SE1 1YW, UK

Nosy Crow and associated logos are trademarks and/or registered
trademarks of Nosy Crow Ltd

Text copyright © Tracey Corderoy, 2013
Cover and illustrations copyright © Joe Berger, 2013

The right of Tracey Corderoy and Joe Berger to be identified
as the author and illustrator respectively of this work has been asserted
by them in accordance with the Copyright, Designs
and Patents Act 1988.

Printed and bound in Turkey

Papers used by Nosy Crow are made from wood grown in
sustainable forests.

ISBN: 978 0 85763 222 7

www.nosycrow.com

CONTENTS

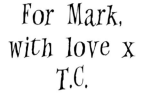

There was nothing Pandora loved more than
spending time with her granny. Araminta
Violet Crow was exciting, funny and kind.
The only tiny problem was you never quite
knew what she'd get up to next. You see,
Pandora's granny was (whisper this next bit)
… *a witch*.

The SPOOKS of CREAKINGTON HALL

Chapter One

Splaaaaaaaat!

A shower of eggs flew across the sitting room and exploded on the spidery wallpaper. One just missed Pandora's head as she peeped round the curtain, looking for Cobweb, Granny's nervous black cat.

Pandora had been helping Granny do some baking when Granny had decided to test her new *Magic*-mix mixer.

5

It hadn't minded the butter, or even the bananas, but it hadn't liked kippers, spell books, or socks. And so it had exploded and Cobweb had shot out of the room to hide.

Suddenly a *booooooooooom* could be heard in the kitchen. What had Granny done *now*?

The kitchen was thick with clouds of fluffy flour when Pandora hurried in.

"Granny!" she coughed. "Oh, Granny – are you OK?"

But Araminta Violet Crow was used
to magical mishaps. "Yes, dear!" came a
cheery voice from deep in the swirling,
white mist. "I'm tickety-boo! And I'll have
this place shipshape in no time!"

Granny peeped out of the floury fog and
Pandora giggled. "Oh, Granny," she said.
"You look funny!"

Granny's hat was spattered with egg
and her cloak was dusted with flour.
Her favourite frog, Croak, was lapping
cake mixture off Granny's bent wand.

"I was just making fairy cakes,"
Granny shrugged, "when those bad-
tempered fairies started throwing the
eggs around! Fairy cakes are meant to
have fairies in them, aren't they?"

Pandora saw three fairies sitting on
top of the dresser, scowling.

Granny poked her tongue out at them, and then, with a swish of her wand, began the magical tidy-up. Her supersonic mop scooted around, sending soft, rainbow bubbles into the air. Pink rubber gloves washed her cake-covered bowls. Feather dusters flicked at the dresser, and the three sulky fairies were dusted away
– *POP! POP! POP!*

"All done!" beamed Granny, when the kitchen was sparkling.

"Nearly," said Pandora, and she pointed to the egg splats on the sitting room wall.

Granny chuckled. "Use your wand, Pip dear. Just magic the mess away!"

11

Pandora bit her lip nervously. She had something to tell Granny. Something she knew that Granny wouldn't like.

Pandora sat Granny down on the sofa and took a deep breath. "I promised Mum I wouldn't do magic," she said. "Not for the whole of half term."

"Oh no!" cried Granny. Then she looked thoughtful. "Was it because of what happened at the library?"

Pandora nodded sadly.

Granny and Pandora, in a moment of reckless fun, had magicked the three little pigs out of their fairy-tale book. Then they'd magicked the big bad wolf out, too (to tell him to be nice to the pigs). Trouble was, he was *starving* and the three "little" pigs were actually very fat and juicy and yummy-looking…

The librarian had called Pandora's parents, who were

"very disappointed" in her and
Granny. Now Pandora wasn't
allowed to do magic for a
whole week!

And so when Pandora's mother, Moonbeam, had dropped her off at Granny's house that morning, she'd told her to "*Be good.*"

Pandora knew this was really code for "*Keep Granny out of trouble…*" But that was easier said than done with a wacky, witchy granny *with a wand*!

Pandora's parents were coming to spend the afternoon with her and Granny. They'd taken time off work especially. But Pandora knew they'd be horrified if all *Granny* wanted to do was have food fights with fairies!

"I think we ought to go out when Mum and Dad get here," said Pandora.

"Out?" replied Granny. "Where?"

"Well," said Pandora, glancing at Granny's newspaper. "How about *here*? Creakington Hall is a big stately home with suits of armour and dungeons and stuff. There's *even* meant to be long-lost treasure. We could go on a treasure hunt!"

Granny's eyes sparkled. "Mmmm…" she said. "Now, that might be fun!"

CREAKINGTON HA

With that, Pandora heard her parents' car pull up outside the house. "Great!" she cried, grabbing Granny's hand. "Let's go!"

Chapter Two

Granny jumped on her broomstick.

"On you get, then!" she smiled. "I can zoom us to Creakington Hall in a jiffy!"

"No! Not on that!" squeaked Pandora's mum, Moonbeam (who *could* do magic but didn't like it).

"Certainly not!" sniffed her dad, Hugo

(who couldn't do magic at all).

With a shrug, Granny re-parked the
broom by the pumpkin patch and hopped
into the car. Pandora sat beside her.

"Come on, then!" called Granny.
"I wonder if they have ghosties at
Creakington Hall. I hope so!"

When they arrived, Granny strode into the house swinging her cauldron-handbag which was belching out clouds of green smoke.

"Did you really need to bring that?" asked Hugo.

"Oh, yes, dear!" beamed Granny. "You never know when you'll fancy a nice cup of gloop!"

They joined a short queue to buy their tickets. As they waited, Granny's hat gave a sudden wiggle, then a frog peeped out from under it.

"R-r-r-ribbit!" croaked
Croak, and he boinged
through the air and landed
on a man's bald head!

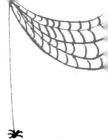

Granny whisked out her wand and magicked him back but the man's wife looked puzzled. "I could have sworn you just grew green hair then, dear."

"*Ridiculous!*" exclaimed her snooty husband.

Moonbeam and Hugo gulped nervously but Pandora had to hold in a giggle. Naughty Croak had left a splat of froggy-poop right on top of the man's shiny bald head!

Pandora gazed around the entrance hall. It looked very tatty and the place smelled of cabbage and damp.

"Psst, *Granny*!" she whispered. "How about we sneak off on our treasure hunt while Mum and Dad look at all the boring stuff?"

"One of our top-secret missions!" beamed Granny. "Oh, yes – I'd *love* to find the treasure!"

"Huh!" came a sneering voice from behind. "Fat chance!"

A freckly boy strode past them, wrinkling his nose at Granny. "If anyone's going to find any treasure, it's me!"

Pandora glared as he marched away. Then things got even worse.

"Let's all take the tour of the house!" cried Moonbeam. "There's so much to see."

Granny and Pandora both sighed. Their top-secret mission to find the treasure had been spoiled.

The tour moved through the house at a snail's pace. Pandora's parents read *every* information card on *every* wall, below *every* painting, beside *every* table and chair. Pandora's dad even made notes!

Granny behaved rather well, apart from
the odd gaping yawn or touching things
she shouldn't. But Pandora knew that
she was getting bored.

And what did Granny
always do when she got
bored? MAGIC...

The tour guide stopped at a portrait of the Fifth Earl of Creakington. He reminded Pandora of a pigeon!

"A friendly little fellow was George," droned the tour guide. "He—"

"—just winked!" boomed a red-faced lady. It was the freckly boy's mother. "That portrait *just winked*!"

"*Ridiculous!*" cried the bald-headed man.

"What would *you* know?!" puffed the lady, her cheeks getting redder by the second. "You with the froggy-poop on your head!"

"*POOPYHEAD!*" sniggered her freckly son.

Pandora looked at Granny, who was tittering behind a pillar. She was up to her old tricks again. Uh oh…

Chapter Three

The tour guide hurried everyone into a
cobwebby dining room. A big chandelier
hung from the ceiling and there were huge
moth-eaten tapestries on the walls. A rusty
suit of armour stood beside the door.

"Hey, *Mum*," hissed Moonbeam. "That
painting back there – did *you* make
George's eyes move?"

"Me?" said Granny, innocently. "Oh, look

at that *wonderful* vase! Come on, Pandora."

Granny dragged Pandora over to a cracked old jug with a missing handle.

"You can't fool me, Granny," Pandora whispered. "I know that winking thing was you."

"OK!" grinned Granny. "But it was just a bit of fun!"

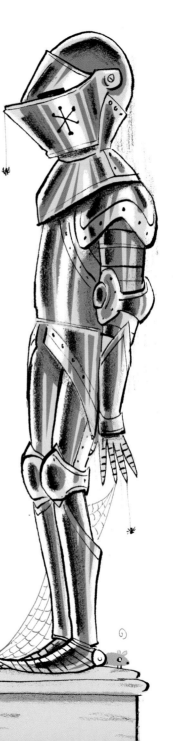

The tour guide pointed to a table that
was laid with a banquet of fake food.
Around it sat dummies in costumes, tucking
in. The guide started droning on again, and
Granny edged her wand from her pocket.
Pandora then heard a faint WHIZZ! POP!
and gasped.

Suddenly, the fake roast pig on the table BURPED very loudly. Then all the dummies started to have a food fight!

A roaring fire shot up in the grate, crackling and popping merrily, and the hundred candles in the old chandelier started burning.

"*What's happening?*" cried the bald-headed man, as the rusty suit of armour gave him a squeaky wave.

Pandora saw the freckly boy looking suspiciously at Granny. She felt sure he'd seen her do magic, and now he was going to tell.

Pandora gulped. To stop Granny getting told off and (shock! horror!) people *staring*, she had to think of something, quick!

"Ghosts!" squeaked Pandora in her most excited voice. "Creakington Hall is *haunted*!"

"Ghosties!" Granny laughed, secretly flicking her wand again. The rusty suit of armour began tottering across the room. As everyone stampeded to the door in fright, Granny's pet frog, Croak, leaped on to her wand, sending random spells shooting out everywhere...

POW! Dusty books flew off their shelves and started flapping about like birds.

PING! The piano in the corner began playing a spooky tune.

BAMM! A stuffed deer-head on the wall shouted, "*BOO!*" then stuck out its tongue and blew a raspberry!

"Ooopsy!" gulped Granny, popping Croak away.

"*Mum!*" shrieked Moonbeam. "Stop this M-A-G-I-C at once!"

Chapter Four

Granny gave her wand a quick flick and the magical mayhem stopped.

"Hang on – where's Alfred?" the tour guide said.

"Who's Alfred?" Pandora asked.

"The suit of armour," explained the guide, crossly. He liked Alfred.

"Not to worry!" Granny piped up. "Alfred's probably just gone for a stroll. And

who could
blame him,
cooped up in here
for centuries!
We'll find
him!"

They checked upstairs, downstairs, and then they looked in the gardens. No Alfred. The tour guide sighed.

"But we still haven't searched the dungeons," said Granny. "Come on!"

She led the way down the gloomy stairs, the star on her wand shining brightly.

"*Ah ha!*" Granny nodded, as they heard a CLANK ... CLANK ... CLANK.

"Alfred!" cried the tour guide with delight, as Alfred clattered around the dark, dusty dungeon.

Granny gave her wand a short, sharp flick and the suit of armour froze in mid-clank. But he was only standing on one leg and looked very *wobbly*!

"Oh, no!" Pandora gasped. "Watch out!"

Everybody held their breath while Alfred teetered and rocked. Then …

… back he tumbled with an enormous CRASH!

When the dust had cleared, they saw that Alfred was in bits. The tour guide looked furious. It would take ages to fit him back together. Then Pandora gave a sudden squeal. "Look!"

Inside Alfred's helmet was a dusty velvet pouch. "Oooh!" said Granny, her eyes now bright. She opened the pouch and…

"Wow!" gasped Pandora, as a dazzling shower of diamonds and thick gold coins rained down on to the floor.

"*Look, everyone — we've found the treasure! Yippee!*"

As a "thank you" all the visitors were treated to a yummy cream cake in the little tearoom. The freckly boy scowled at Pandora.

"Huh! If my granny were a witch," he said, "*I'd* have found that treasure first."

Pandora didn't argue but reached for Granny's wand and gave it a secret little flick. Suddenly, the boy's cake turned into a big slimy toad.

"Ha!" Pandora giggled. "Serves you right!"

The GLORIOUS GRANNY BAKE OFF!

Chapter One

"*Goodness!*" cried Granny. "So many cloaks! Which one, Pip dear? Which one?"

Pandora peered into the wardrobe. All of Granny's cloaks were black. "Maybe, um, a *black* one?" she shrugged.

Granny took out a long black cloak and threw it around her shoulders. Cobweb the cat gave a nervous, "*Miaaaaaow!*"

"He says I look like a giant bat!" chuckled

Granny.

Granny wanted to look nice today because she and her two (whisper it!) *witchy* friends were going to be on TV! *The Glorious Granny Bake Off* was a programme where grannies competed to see whose baking was best.

The programme was very popular. All of Pandora's friends watched it. So did all of her teachers.

Each granny was allowed to take along one helper. And Granny had chosen Pandora!

Pandora was worried. What if she dropped all the eggs by accident, or set the studio on fire? Uh oh...

Granny tied up her cloak. "Time to go!" she said, popping her wand into her pocket.

"But, Granny, there's no magic allowed!" said Pandora.

"I know," Granny nodded. "But I always like to have my wand, just in case!"

When they arrived at the TV station Granny's friends, Gwendolyn and Tilda, were already there with their helpers, meanie Merlin and snooty Opal.

The two grannies were having great fun magicking on their make-up. Hairbrushes and lipsticks were flying around all over the place!

Opal and Merlin eyed Pandora as if she was a nasty sea-slug. Pandora ignored them, and she and Granny sat down to have their make-up put on.

Pandora *hated* the powder, which made her sneeze and her skin come out in a red spotty rash. "Ow!"

Everyone was then shown into the studio which had been made to look like a fancy kitchen. The producer told them what they had to do.

"First you must bake your favourite cakes. Then you must make Chef Edwardo's world-famous pudding for him. And remember: NO MAGIC ALLOWED!"

"OK!" beamed the grannies. It was time. Pandora swallowed hard. Fingers crossed all her friends' TVs weren't working today!

Chapter Two

The grannies and their helpers were shown to their tables.

"OK," said the producer. "*Action!*"

Granny had decided to bake butterfly cakes. Pandora weighed out the ingredients and only dropped *one* thing. Unfortunately, it was a huge bag of flour and it exploded all over her.

"Don't worry," said Granny. "It hides

your rash *beautifully*, dear!"

As Granny got on with her mixing, Pandora eyed the others. Tilda was baking a lemon sponge and Gwendolyn's carrot cake was well underway. Merlin was a whizz with the carrot peeler and Opal was *born* to squeeze lemons.

Tilda iced her lemon sponge with sparkly icing, while Gwendolyn covered her cake with fancy carrot-shaped sweets.

Either they had been practising, thought Pandora, or they baked without magic *a lot* because their cakes looked very yummy indeed.

Granny's cakes didn't look *nearly* so good. They were rather lopsided and burned round the edges.

"It's OK!" beamed Granny. "I'm not finished yet!"

On the windowsill behind her was a pot of flowers covered in big, bright butterflies.

She opened the window, brought in the pot and then popped some butterflies on to her cakes.

"Ta-daaaa!" she beamed. "What better to have on butterfly cakes than butterflies!"

The judges bustled up, tutting. "*Real* butterflies are not allowed!"

"Oh," said Granny, looking glum.

61

The judges then awarded their scores. Tilda's lemon sponge was the winner and Gwendolyn's carrot cake came second. Sadly, Granny's butterfly cakes were disqualified.

Next it was the show-stopping pudding. Chef Edwardo swept in with his famous pudding and Pandora gulped.

It was a big, fancy swan made from swirls of fluffy meringue.

It had wings, a long neck and a dainty white face. Its eyes were made from liquorice circles and it had two crisp ginger biscuits for a beak.

No way would her granny *EVER* make this!

They were doomed.

Chapter Three

Granny was having *such* trouble with her swan. She whisked and whisked the egg mixture but it wouldn't make "stiff peaks" when she prodded it with her fork.

"Maybe I should add some glue?" she suggested.

Pandora shook her head. "You can't put *glue* in food, Granny."

Granny sighed.

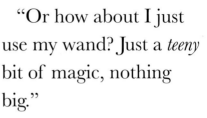

"Or how about I just use my wand? Just a *teeny* bit of magic, nothing big."

Pandora shook her head again. "No magic!"

Pandora glanced over at the other grannies. Their mixture had LOADS of stiff peaks! Maybe Opal and Merlin were better helpers?

Granny slopped the mixture out of her bowl and it made a runny puddle on her plate.

"Maybe if we add more sugar?" said Pandora. Granny shrugged.

Pandora headed off

to the larder but stopped sharp just outside.
Somebody was already in there. Pandora
peeped around the door and gasped.

Opal was waving her wand over some
eggs and muttering *a magical helping spell…*

"Little eggs, all round and
white, make my granny's
swan so bright!"

Opal was cheating. So *that's* why her granny was doing so well!

Pandora shrank behind the door as Opal dashed back to the kitchen with the eggs and Merlin raced into the larder.

Pandora watched as Merlin swished his wand over a jar of sugar and commanded it to give *his* granny's swan fine wings! Then he was off back to the kitchen with the jar of magic sugar.

Pandora couldn't believe it. "*How piggily unfair!*" she scowled. Opal *and* Merlin had been cheating all along!

Pandora stomped into the larder, grabbed a jar of sugar, then thundered back to the kitchen. If *they* could magically help their grannies *so could she*!

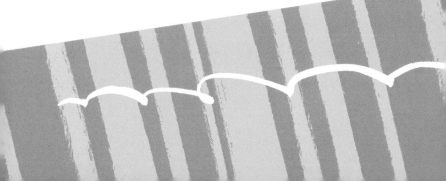

"Sprinkle some of this on to your mixture!" Pandora said to Granny at once.

"But I'm really not sure it will help, dear."

"I am," Pandora nodded. "I'm *very* sure."

Granny sighed. "All right then," she said, and she started to sprinkle on the sugar. As she did, Pandora edged Granny's wand out of her pocket and whispered…

"Fluffy white wings and a neck so tall – make *my* granny's swan the best one of all!"

POOF!

A swirl of magical stars puffed out of the end of the wand. Quickly, Pandora fanned them away. But somebody had seen…

"*Cheat!*" shrieked Opal, pointing at Pandora.

Pandora jumped and, quite by accident, *another* spell burst from the wand. It sent three little eggs zooming through the air, then…

SPLAT! SPLAT! SPLAT!

The eggs landed on Gwendolyn's head. Gwendolyn looked very surprised.

Then a grin spread across her face.

"Oh, goody!" she chuckled. "Food-fight time!"

"Did someone say *food-fight*?" Granny
beamed.

"*Splendid!*" Tilda cried.

All three grannies grabbed their wands.
Then together they uttered the food-fight
spell…

"SPLATTTIOCIOUS!"

Pandora dived for cover as (take a deep breath) eggs-and-flour-and-sugar-and-lemons-and-carrots-and-lopsided-cakes-and-butter-and-milk-and-dribbles-of-sloppy-wet-swan went flying through the air.

"Stop!" yelled the producer. "STOP!"

Chapter Four

"*Arrrgggh!*"

The producer slipped on some butter and landed head first in Gwendolyn's swan.

"Pffff!" he spluttered.

"Look!" giggled Opal.

"Ha ha!" laughed Merlin.

And even Pandora snorted.

The producer had wings shooting out of his head, as if he'd grown pixie ears! And the swan's head was sitting on top of his own, like a hat.

Now everyone was plastered in egg and flour but nobody seemed to care. This was *way* more fun than baking any day!

Granny decided to turn Tilda's meringue swan into a *real* one, just for fun. But it turned out to be *really* grumpy.

When the producer tried to catch it, the swan started nipping his bottom.

NIP!

NIP-NIP!

NIP!

NIP!

"Noooo!" he cried.

The Glorious Granny Bake Off had finished.
No one had won but none of the grannies
cared.

With a swish of their wands they cleaned up the mess. They were starting to feel a bit bad about the producer but he'd disappeared.

"Maybe he's still being chased by that swan?" grinned Pandora.

It was time to go home. But just as they were

about to zoom off on their broomsticks, the producer suddenly popped up. Pandora could see a bit of beak left on the top of his head.

"Oh, hello dear!" beamed the grannies.

"Sorry about the swan," gulped Pandora.

"Never mind about that!" the producer smiled. "Hundreds of viewers have rung in to say they really loved the show! So how about, well – doing MORE? *The Glorious Granny Knit Off … The Glorious Granny Shop Off* – a new thing every time!"

"With magic?" asked Granny.

"Definitely!" the producer cried.

All three grannies agreed at once. It was going to be a hoot! Then they all zoomed off home for tea.

"Shall I bake us a pie, dear?" Granny asked, as they flew over the town.

But Pandora had had enough *baking*! "What about fish and chips?" she said.

So that's just what they did. They stopped in the park and ate them by the pond.

"When I do my programmes," said Granny, "I shall need a little *helper*, you know."

Pandora nearly choked on a chip.

Uh oh…

ALAKAZOOM! The BIG BUNNY BOOM!

Chapter One

"Dead," Nellie nodded, lifting up a limp carrot stalk.

"We'll lose the gardening competition," Clover sniffed.

"No, we won't," said Pandora. "My carrots are just a bit poorly, that's all!"

Pandora and her friends were at their after-school gardening club. It was run by a wacky (whisper it!) *witch* called Araminta

Violet Crow. And she was Pandora's granny.

For weeks the club had been growing fruit and vegetables for a big competition that was being judged the next day.

The prize for the best fruit and vegetables was a school trip to Beanstalk Land, a super-cool farm with an adventure playground in the shape of a giant beanstalk!

Pandora sighed and plodded off to tell Granny about the poorly carrots. As she waited in the cobwebby potting shed, Granny swept in. She was carrying a tray of pansies that all seemed to have grown little faces!

"Um, Granny," Pandora said, "have you *done* anything to those flowers?"

"Like what?" grinned Granny, quickly slipping her wand back into her cloak pocket. The pansies poked out their tongues at Pandora and giggled.

"Granny," said Pandora. "My carrots are looking a tiny bit … ill."

"Not any more!" Granny smiled. "I just whizzed them up a drink and now they're fine!"

"Really?" smiled Pandora. "Thanks a lot!"

But suddenly she remembered Peter, Granny's prize pumpkin. Once Granny had whizzed Peter up a get-well drink. It had been a fizzy pink *growing potion*. Five minutes later, Peter was the size of a gorilla!

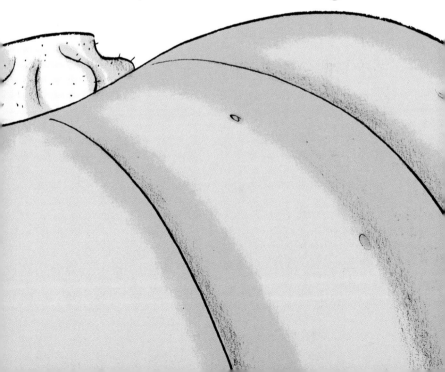

"Eeek!" squeaked Pandora, jumping
to her feet. "Was the drink you gave my
carrots, sort of … pink?"

"Err…" muttered Granny. "Oh, golly – is
it home time *already*?!"

Granny dashed outside, grabbed her
broomstick and they both climbed on.

Pandora still looked worried as she put on

her helmet.

"But, Granny, using magic is cheat—"

"Got your lunchbox?" Granny butted in.

"Yes, but—"

"*Good!* And your reading book?"

"Yes," said Pandora. "But what about my *carrots*?"

"Off we go!" beamed Granny. "Hold on tight!"

As they whizzed home through the fluffy clouds Pandora was still thinking about her carrots.

What if Granny *had* fed them fizzy pink potion? Yikes!

Chapter Two

The next morning Granny Crow whooshed down Pandora's chimney.

"Mum," Pandora's mother sighed. "You really should use the door."

"We might have lit a fire!" tutted Pandora's dad.

"Oh, Granny – you're all sooty!" giggled Pandora.

Granny cleaned her sooty clothes with a

flick of her wand. Then they all sat down to breakfast. Granny magicked up a jar of beetlecurrant jam and spread a thick, black dollop on her toast. She took a big bite and Pandora shuddered.

"Mmmm," smiled Granny, licking her lips. *"Delicious!"*

After breakfast, Pandora's parents left for work and Pandora told Granny about Plop.

Plop had been the class goldfish. But last week he'd sadly died. Plop had never done much except swim (and plop) but he'd been very nice all the same.

BEETLE-CURRANT JAM

"Oh!" said Granny. "So you need a new class pet!"

She wiggled her wand and a shower of stars shot out of the end... BANG!

Pandora peered through the starry smoke

to see a cute baby dragon on the rug. "Ta-daa!" beamed Granny. The baby dragon gave a little hiccup and giant flames shot out of his nostrils.

"But Granny," gasped
Pandora. "My teacher
won't let us have a
dragon."

Grumbling, Granny vanished the dragon away then put out all the fires he had started. Luckily her wand made a very good hosepipe!

"Right," said Granny, finally. "Time to go to school!"

It was going to be a very big day. Granny had lots of flowers to plant before the judges arrived. She wanted to make Pandora's school look tip-top.

When they got there, the playground was packed with shouty children. Granny's gardening club raced across to Pandora.

"We're going to win today!" cried Jake.

"Yes!" grinned Nellie. "Come and see your carrots!"

Bluebell opened the garden gate and they whisked Pandora inside.

They passed Jake's nice,
firm runner beans.

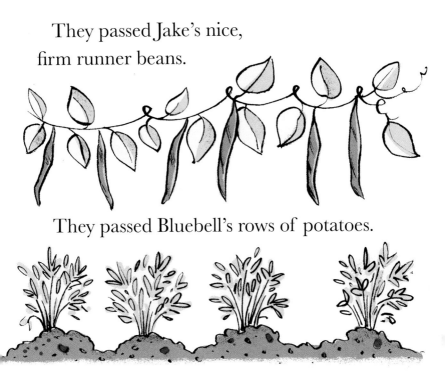

They passed Bluebell's rows of potatoes.

They passed Nellie's strawberries and
Clover's raspberries, all looking lovely and
juicy.

Finally they came to the carrot patch. Pandora stopped and gasped.

"OH, NO!"

Yesterday the carrot tops had been floppy and small but *now* they looked like giant bushy squirrel tails! And the carrots looked ready to burst out of the ground!

What had Granny *done*! When the judges saw those carrot tops they were *bound* to say they'd cheated! Then everyone would (shock! horror!) *stare*...

Chapter Three

Ding-a-ling-a-ling!

The school bell rang and everyone skipped in. Except Pandora.

She was rummaging inside her school bag for her wand and muttering to herself. "I need to magic these carrots smaller, right now!"

Then she remembered that she'd used her wand to magic her teeth clean that morning. She must have left it on the bathroom sink. "Oh, no!"

Sighing, Pandora plodded into the classroom and plonked herself down next to Nellie.

First there was a maths test. Then they all wrote a story. But poor Pandora couldn't stop thinking about *carrots*…

Pandora's teacher marked their tests.

"Pandora Isabella Podmore!" he frowned,

waving her book in the air. "Nineteen minus eight does *not* equal carrot!"

$$19 - 8 = \text{🥕}$$

"Sorry, Mr Bibble!" gulped Pandora.

"*And*," he scowled, prodding her story, "you were meant to write about the *Romans*, not *carrots*!"

"And look!" giggled Bluebell. "She's drawn a *carrot* instead of a *chariot*!"

After lunch, it was time for the judging of the gardening competition.

Pandora's knees knocked as Mr Grimly, the head teacher, brought in the three judges. One of them was tall and skinny, and looked like a runner bean. The other wore a thick brown suit, as hairy as a coconut! The lady judge was short and round, and reminded Pandora of a turnip.

They walked along the nice clean path, past the neat flowerbeds. As they did, Granny's pansies grinned like Cheshire cats.

"Such happy specimens!" the lady judge smiled. Granny blushed.

The judges
arrived at
Jake's runner beans
and picked one off the plant. "Hmmm,
very good!" said the tall, skinny judge.
Next, Bluebell dug up a few of her
potatoes and the judges
examined them closely.
"Wonderful shape!" the
round lady judge nodded.
They loved Nellie's
strawberries and

Clover's raspberries too. Then finally they came to Pandora's carrots…

"Oh!" said the judge in the hairy brown suit. "What an enormous carrot top!" And he prodded the bushy green leaves with the tip of his pencil.

As he did, the ground beneath the stalk gave a little rumble. Then a whopper of a carrot shot up out of it – POP!

The carrot soared high into the air like a great muddy rocket, showering everyone below in dirt and worms.

"Arggh!" screamed the judges, as the giant carrot turned and dropped back down to earth. It crash-landed beside Granny with an enormous thud! Then *all* the massive carrots underground blasted off...

POP!
POP! POP!
POP!

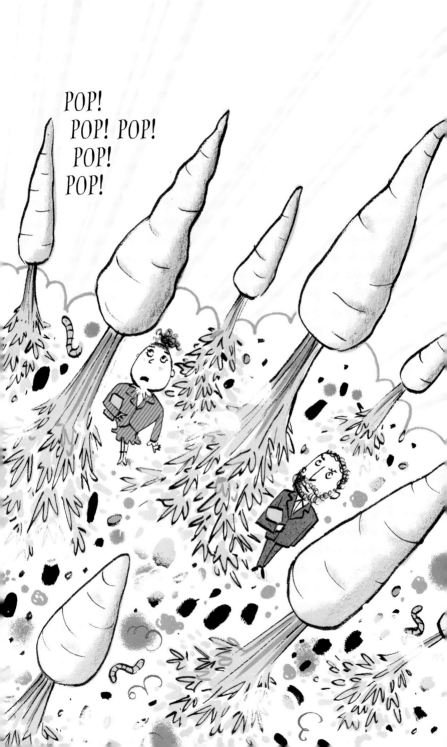

Chapter Four

When the downpour of mud and creepy-crawlies was over, Mr Grimly looked fit to explode.

"Disgraceful!" muttered the lady judge. "*Magic* in a gardening competition! This school is disqualified!"

"But…" shrugged Granny. "I only gave the carrots a *drink*."

The whole school peered into the garden,

now littered with ginormous carrots. Pandora blushed. "Granny, please put things right!" she whispered.

Granny nodded and whisked her wand from her cloak. Mr Grimly backed away nervously.

Granny gave her wand a twizzly flick and a swirl of starry mist shot out. Granny's spell quickly whisked the giant carrots into a tall, neat pile. Then it made the potting-shed door spring open – *PING!*

Three sweeping brushes came dancing out, followed by some spades and trowels. Bringing up the rear was a wheelbarrow filled with bright sunflowers.

As the brushes swept the paths clean, the spades shovelled soil into the giant holes made by the exploding carrots.

Finally the trowels neatly planted the sunflowers where Pandora's carrots had been.

"But..." Mr Grimly spluttered. "What about those giant carrots!"

Granny flicked her wand again. In a puff of smoke a huge rabbit appeared. "Giant carrots need a giant rabbit to *nibble* them!" beamed Granny.

The rabbit bounded over to the carrots and started nibbling like mad.

"He's cute," Nellie nodded.

"He's greedy!" said Bluebell.

"*We like him!*" chorused Clover and Jake. Pandora liked him, too. Very much!

When the giant rabbit had polished off
the carrots Granny waved her wand *again*.
WHIZZ! POP!

Now the rabbit became a teeny-weeny
bunny with the *floppiest* ears, the *fluffiest* tail
and the *twitchiest* nose in the world!

"Meet your new class pet!" grinned
Granny.

"Oh!" smiled Pandora. But Granny
hadn't *quite* finished yet.

Because they'd lost the competition,
there'd be no school trip to Beanstalk Land.
So Granny waved her wand one final time
and Jake's runner beans began to grow.

Out of the garden they twisted and twirled, around the field they swooped and swirled, then up, up, up they soared into the sky!

They grew into an *amazing* adventure playground! "Wow!" gasped everyone. It was just like Beanstalk Land!

Cheering, everyone bounded off to play. All except Pandora, who was cuddling the little bunny.

"Nibble looks hungry again," she said, as he nibbled the end of her sleeve.

Granny looked. "So he does! I'll whizz him up big, juicy carrot!"

"No!" cried Pandora. Then she giggled. "Well, maybe just a *small* one, Granny…"

The End

Look out for more
magical mayhem from
Pandora and her
wacky granny!